To Alice, Jocelyn and Reuben,
with love – TK

Especially for Lucas
– DW

Sandy Creek
NEW YORK

An Imprint of Sterling Publishing
387 Park Avenue South
New York, NY 10016

SANDY CREEK and the distinctive Sandy Creek logo are registered trademarks of Barnes & Noble, Inc. Text © 2011 by Timothy Knapman. Illustrations © 2011 by David Walker. First published in the United Kingdom by Macmillan Publishers Ltd. This 2013 edition published by Sandy Creek. All rights reserved.

Written by
Timothy Knapman

Illustrated by
David Walker

The GREAT EASTER EGG SCRAMBLE

Sandy Creek
NEW YORK

It's Easter Bunny's party today
And all his friends are on their way.

He's made them cakes and buns and sweets,
Ice cream, fudge, and chocolate treats!

Look, swings and slides to play on too.
A merry-go-round – so much to do!

Then he lifts a cloth and sees, with a shiver . . .

. . . the basket of eggs he was meant to deliver!

He gets on his whizzy-wheeled, super-quick bike
And scrambles off down the road, fast as you like!

"Brown is for Chicken, Duck's shell is blue.
The green egg is meant for Mrs. Emu.

Crocodile's is yellow, Turtle's is white.
And the egg for the Penguins is cold – yes, that's right!"

Let's hope Easter Bunny won't scramble the rhyme.

"Brown is for Emu . . . Oh, look at the time!"

"Mrs. Chicken!
I'm sorry I'm late," Bunny cries.

"Thanks for the egg," she says.
"My, what a size!"

She sits down to warm it: she knows what to do.
It hatches and out comes . . .

A BABY EMU!

But Bunny is off and he's reached Mrs. Duck.

"You've brought me an egg, Easter Bunny, what luck!"

But a duck egg's not yellow and big as a rock.

And when it cracks open . . .

Great snakes!

Now the Emus are happy. "An egg," they both sigh.
But their little house is all tidy and dry.

How will they feel when they find their new daughter's
A TURTLE who splashes the whole place with water?

Mrs. Crocodile's sunning herself by the river,
When Bunny calls by with an egg to deliver.

It's blue and it's small, and was that a cluck?
What have you given her, Bunny?

"The egg for the Turtles is cold – is that right?

Hot ones or cold ones, they're all a delight!"

But then the egg opens and – oh deary me!

Out strides . . .

. . . A PENGUIN, as proud as can be!

Quick! The last of the eggs is beginning to hatch . . .

"No time to stop, sorry Penguins, here –

catch!"

And off Bunny rides. "I've a party to run!
Come along later, you're sure to have fun!"

Then the egg splits apart and the Penguins both shout,

As – WOW! – a poor frozen CHICKEN pops out!

So everyone's got the wrong baby,
Oh dear!

And no one's enjoying the party, that's clear.

It's up to Bunny to sort out this mess.

He says, "Onto the merry-go-round, children, yes!"

He gives it a spin . . .

they go whizzing past . . .

Now everyone's got the right baby . . .

. . . at last!